DISAPPEARING ACT

Dayle Campbell Gaetz

RAVEN BOOKS
an imprint of
ORCA BOOK PUBLISHERS

Library and Archives Canada Cataloguing in Publication

Gaetz, Dayle, 1947–, author
Disappearing act / Dayle Campbell Gaetz.
(Rapid Reads)

Issued also in print and electronic formats.
ISBN 978-1-4598-0822-5 (pbk.).—ISBN 978-1-4598-0823-2 (pdf).—
ISBN 978-1-4598-0824-9 (epub)

I. Title. II. Series: Rapid reads
PS8563.A25317D57 2015   C813'.54   C2015-901569-0
2015-901570-4

First published in the United States, 2015
Library of Congress Control Number: 2014935365

Summary: In this murder mystery, Leena O'Neil, a young woman
who is working to become a private investigator, works to clear her
sister in her first case. (RL 4.2)

*Orca Book Publishers is dedicated to preserving the environment and has
printed this book on Forest Stewardship Council® certified paper.*

Orca Book Publishers gratefully acknowledges the support for
its publishing programs provided by the following agencies:
the Government of Canada through the Canada Book Fund and the
Canada Council for the Arts, and the Province of British Columbia
through the BC Arts Council and the Book Publishing Tax Credit.

Cover design by Jenn Playford
Cover photography by iStock Photo

ORCA BOOK PUBLISHERS
PO Box 5626, Stn. B
Victoria, BC Canada
V8R 6S4

ORCA BOOK PUBLISHERS
PO Box 468
Custer, WA USA
98240-0468

www.orcabook.com
Printed and bound in Canada.

18 17 16 15 • 4 3 2 1

DISAPPEARING
ACT

*To my mom, who is nothing like
Leena O'Neil's mother and who never tried
to force me into law school.*

ONE

Anything to do with private investigations grabbed my interest. Always has. That's why I stood staring at a sink full of grungy dishes, waiting for an important interview on my radio. Should I start washing or sit down and take notes?

"How to disappear." A deep male voice broke into my thoughts. *"I spent twenty years as a private detective tracking down fugitives. I know every trick in the book."*

"And you've explained them all in your new book, Without a Trace," the female interviewer said with a laugh.

"I could write my own book," I muttered, turning on the tap. "I'd call it *Disappearing for Dummies*." Because seriously, if I could do it, anyone with half a brain could too.

"It's not easy," the detective said, contradicting me. *"You'll spend the rest of your life glancing over your shoulder, hiding from all those people trying to track you down."*

I glanced over my shoulder. No one peering through the window, no one lurking in the shadows.

"People get caught because they get sloppy," the detective continued. *"They can't let go of old habits, like eating sushi every Friday night, hanging out at the racetrack or collecting rare books. Change your lifestyle and they won't know where to look."*

"Or be like me—change nothing and no one bothers looking," I said.

"In my experience, most folks are relieved to get caught," he went on. *"They often thanked*

me for finding them because they were so tired of running."

"But if someone seriously wants to disappear?" the interviewer asked. *"You know, because they're being stalked or something? What advice do you have for them?"*

"Okay. Number one. Plan ahead. Know exactly where you're going, and take enough money to get there."

"So," I said to the radio. I wiped the countertop and dropped my damp sponge in the cluttered sink. Turned off the tap. "Three years ago I walked out the door with a backpack, a shoulder bag and sixty-seven dollars and twenty-three cents. How's that for planning ahead?"

"Two. Set up a new identity ahead of time, so you can find a job, open a bank account, that sort of thing."

I wandered over to the table. "I hitched a ride to the island, changed my name from

Colleen, which I hate, to Leena, which feels like me, and that's it. Kept my old bank account and got a job under my own name. How am I doing so far?"

"Three. Cut off all ties, ditch your smartphone, get rid of your Facebook and Twitter accounts, wipe out your email addresses."

"At least we agree on something. I stopped using Facebook and changed my email address when I switched providers, but I kept my old phone. Because you never know, one day my family might try to find me."

So far, no one had reported me missing. But to be fair, they may not have noticed I was gone. Mother always said I was too quiet for my own good. Maybe she was right.

"Four," the detective continued. *"Never call your mother, girlfriend, sister or anyone else from a traceable phone. Never."*

"Okay. Got that covered." I knew what would happen if I called my mother. She'd

4

put me on hold. Either that or ask me to call back later. Same for my sister. Been there. Done that.

My back pocket blared out a Rhino ringtone. I grabbed my phone on the second ring. Stared at the screen. *Gina!* Typical. I say my sister would never talk to me, and two seconds later she's proving me wrong. Gina was always the perfect one. The sister who could do no wrong, who was never too quiet. Gina was the smart one with the perfect career, the perfect husband, the perfect life. If Gina went missing, everyone would notice.

The phone rang again, shivering in my hand. My finger hovered over the screen. Push up to answer. Push down to decline. I dropped the phone on the table and sprinted over to the radio. Switched it off.

My phone rang a fourth and final time. I remained by the radio—tense, waiting. Finally, I sauntered back. Picked up the phone. Checked for voice messages.

"Colleen?" The voice sounded too uncertain to be Gina's. My older sister was always confident. Always in charge. Never quite approving of me. Gina looked and acted so much like our mother, I used to tell my friends she was a clone. I never mentioned that I came from another planet, but for a while there, I believed it. Must have been all that science fiction I read before getting hooked on crime novels.

"Are you there?" the voice asked. "It's me, Georgia."

Georgia? Who the hell was Georgia?

"Your sister," she added. "Georgina."

My sister changed her name too?

After a pause she continued, so softly I strained to hear. The only word I caught was "Colleen" and it grated on my nerves. I had almost forgotten Colleen. The girl I never wanted to be. The girl I left home to escape.

I shuffled to the window, folded my arms across my stomach and stared out at my garden. One lonesome lawn chair, maples turning golden on top while brilliant yellow chrysanthemums clustered at their feet. I thought of the chrysanthemums I'd planted in my mother's garden. Had anyone watered them? Were they blooming now too? Yellow chrysanthemums were my favorite autumn flower.

I replayed the message with the phone pressed tight to my ear. *"Please, Colleen, I need your help. Call me. Please."* Her voice faded to nothing.

I sank onto the nearest chair. "So, you finally call me because you need help?" I asked aloud. "Please tell me why I should care."

Leaving my phone, I slammed out of the house. But her voice followed me down the long, winding driveway, sounding more desperate with every step. I need your help. Call me. Please.

I stopped. Turned around. Started back. I'd run away once, but never again. I wasn't a kid anymore. It was time to face up to my family, and the desperate tone of Gina's voice told me she really needed my help. I had to find out what was wrong. I threw open the door and grabbed the phone. It started ringing in my hand. "Gina?" I answered, my heart crashing into my lungs.

"Georgia," she corrected, uncompromising as always. "I'm catching the next ferry. Meet me. *Please.* Don't call again. Take the battery out of your phone."

"Why?" I asked. But she was gone.

TWO

The little car ferry eased into the dock, pushing a wave of white water that sloshed around the pilings below me. My sister was almost here. I felt ill.

Be nice, I reminded myself. Don't let her get to you. No longer the angry nineteen-year-old who'd dropped out of university and left home in a snit, I would be kind, tactful and mature.

Foot passengers disembarked first, making their way single file up a narrow ramp. An old man leaning heavily on two canes took the lead. He looked in danger of toppling over. Two teenage boys stomped at his heels in their youthful haste. I held my breath as the boys moved to either side of the old man, then breathed again when each took an arm and helped him gently to the top.

A young mother followed, carrying a sleepy baby and towing a wailing toddler by the hand. Then came a second passenger leaning on a cane, her age difficult to determine. Her head was bowed, her face hidden by the brim of an orange baseball cap. She held the silver cane awkwardly in her right hand and dragged her right leg with every step. In her left hand was a large white plastic shopping bag. A tote bag was slung across her chest from right shoulder to left hip. Her oversized blue sweatshirt hung loosely over baggy Capri pants. Her clothing was so wrinkled, it had to be fresh from the white shopping bag. Orange Crocs completed her outfit, a match for her baseball cap. My ultra-style-conscious sister would gag at the sight. Good thing she wasn't next in line. Come to think of it, where was she?

I watched the last foot passenger step onto the ramp. A young woman clutching both handrails, struggling to pull herself up the steep ramp on heels like stilts and a skirt so short it was barely worth wearing.

"Shall we go?"

The harsh whisper made me jump. I turned and stared into the face below the orange baseball cap, eyes hidden behind dark glasses. "Gina?

"Shh," she whispered, glancing around. "It's Georgia, not Gina. Can't you remember that?"

I cringed. No sisterly hug. No asking how I was doing. No regrets over how long it'd been. But seriously, what did I expect?

"Nice outfit, *Georgia*. Tell me, is this the in look for fall?" So much for the new, mature me. But she started it, right?

She winced as she lifted the bulging tote bag from her shoulder and handed it to me. "Where's your car?"

Fuming, I slipped the heavy tote over my shoulder, left the plastic shopping bag to her and walked just fast enough that she had to hurry. I didn't ask why she was limping. Or why she was using a golf club as a cane. At that moment I didn't care.

We tossed her bags into the trunk of my ancient brown Toyota. For a moment I watched my sister struggle, wincing with pain, to ease herself into the passenger seat. Then I broke down and went to help. The loose sleeve of her shirt fell back and exposed a dark purple bruise on her arm, above a red and swollen wrist. I also noticed long scrapes, red and inflamed, covering her right leg below the knee. I closed the door and walked around to the driver's side.

"What happened?" I asked as we pulled out of the parking lot and started up the hill.

"I fell off my bike."

"Ouch! I hope you were wearing a helmet."

"Of course." Her tone dismissed my question. I knew what she was thinking. *I'm the perfect one, remember? The one who does everything right.*

"It's slightly demolished," she admitted, a quaver in her voice.

I waited.

"Someone tried to run me off the road."

"What? But Gina—are you sure?"

She sighed. Translation—*It's Georgia, not Gina. Can't you remember that?*

"I'm sure it was Mark," she said.

"Mark? Your husband?"

I glanced at my sister. Georgia. When had she changed her name? She stared straight ahead, stone-faced.

Of course, Mark her husband. Stupid question. I should have known better. "But why would he do that?"

Georgia yanked off the baseball cap, ran her fingers through her short auburn hair and looked out her side window. "Simple. He wants to get rid of me so he can move into our house with his girlfriend."

I opened my mouth to ask, "Are you sure?" But before one word slipped out, my mother's voice invaded my brain. *Think before you speak, Colleen.*

Rounding a sharp right corner, we headed away from the harbor while I struggled to find the right words. Words that wouldn't make my sister sigh, glare or snap at me. As it turned out, silence was the best policy.

She flopped against the headrest and exhaled a puff of air. "A couple of months ago I discovered Mark was having an affair with some bimbo waitress next to his office. Can you imagine?"

I shook my head. Pressed my lips together. Could not imagine.

"Naturally, I kicked him out of the house."

Naturally.

"I thought he'd move in with her, but he found an apartment close to town. He keeps phoning and texting me. He says he loves me and wants to try again."

I waited.

"I don't believe him. It's not me he wants, it's the house. And then there's the little matter of the loan."

"Loan? What loan?"

Georgia hesitated. Sighed. Seemed to make up her mind. "Shortly after we got married, I loaned Mark some money to help him and his partner purchase the Volkswagen dealership in town. If we divorce, I demand my money back right now." She snapped her fingers. "But with me out of the way, he would get to keep everything, including the house—he could move into it with his little girlfriend."

I didn't know what to say. Georgia had it all figured out. Her husband had tried to kill her so he could live happily ever after. But it wasn't like my sister to run away from trouble—that was more my style. "When did the accident happen?" I asked.

"It was no accident."

I drove on, past an apple orchard on the right, a run-down farmhouse on the left.

"A couple of days ago. I always ride my bike on Sundays, and Mark knows that. But it wasn't the first attempt on my life."

I waited for more, but she fell silent. At the top of a long, straight hill, I turned up the unpaved, twisting driveway that leads to my small rented home. In the deep shade of the tall cedars that line the drive, I glanced at my sister's face. It was wet with tears.

THREE

Georgia dropped her shopping bag on the bench inside my back door. Leaning heavily on the head of her golf-club cane, she studied the open space of my modular home. The narrow, L-shaped kitchen with fake-oak cabinets and scratched, outdated countertops. The round table beside a window that overlooked my garden, dark now in evening shadow.

Behind the kitchen was my living room. A blue velveteen sofa and two unmatched chairs faced an entertainment center that held my computer and TV.

"So," she said, "this little *trailer* was worth running away from home for?"

I dropped the tote at her feet. "*Georgia,* I would quite happily live in a tent to escape your constant criticism. Yours and Mom's."

For once in our lives my sister was struck silent. She stood there for a moment, as if waiting for an apology she was not going to get—for once in our lives. Then she hobbled through the kitchen, making good use of her cane and wincing with every step. Every good lawyer is an expert at playing for sympathy. I knew this. Sadly, it too often works.

"Listen, Georgia," I said. "I didn't ask you to come here. You begged for my help, remember? Say the word and I'll gladly take you right back to the ferry." I checked the time on my microwave. "If we leave now, you can catch the next ferry—which, by the way, is the last one today."

She sank onto the sofa. Placed the club-cane across her lap. Stared at the blank TV screen. "You're right," she whispered. Then, even more quietly, "I'm sorry."

I stared at the back of her head. At her stunningly bad haircut. Had I imagined it, or did my sister really apologize?

"So I'm guessing you're staying the night," I said. "In that case I'll start dinner. You probably won't believe this, but I'm an awesome cook."

"You always did like to cook," she said, her voice so flat I didn't know if her words were meant as an insult or a compliment.

"While dinner's cooking, we can have a glass of wine—if you promise not to complain that it's not up to your standards."

She sat quietly while I prepared my favorite baked-tetrazzini recipe and put it in the oven. Then I grabbed some warmed pita, homemade hummus, two wine glasses and a bottle of my best inexpensive red wine. I joined her on the sofa.

"This looks good," she mumbled. "I'm starving."

A few sips and a couple of nibbles later, I posed one of the questions forming a long queue in my brain. "So what's the story on the golf club? Is that the latest thing in cane design? Personalized canes for the upwardly mobile?"

Her lips twitched, and for a second I thought she might laugh. "My nine iron was handy," she said, "and exactly the right height. My leg's a bit sore, as you can see." She sipped her wine, rolled it on her tongue, swallowed. "You know, that's actually not half bad."

"I'll take that as a compliment." I swallowed a massive gulp. "What's the deal with your clothes? I never thought you'd be caught dead in such an outfit."

"*Dead* being the operative word here." She managed a small, twisted smile. "As it turns out, I prefer staying alive over wearing the latest fashion."

"So you went straight for hideous," I said.

Georgia glanced at me, gave one brief snort of laughter, then turned serious. "Since we're playing Twenty Questions, what's with calling yourself *Leena*?" She said my name like a dirty word.

"As I'm sure you never bothered to notice," I said, holding back anger, "I always hated the name Colleen. To me, it sounds harsh and critical. So I dropped the *C-o-l* and added an *a*. Leena makes me feel happy."

A twist of her lips, the tiniest of shrugs. She reached for her wineglass.

"Kind of like shortening Georgina to Gina," I pointed out. "Which is what we called you for years."

"Nothing like that," she snapped. "Leena isn't even a real name."

"But now you want to be Georgia?"

"If you hadn't run away you'd know I finally worked up the nerve to change my name to Georgia in spite of what Mother thinks. Georgia is a power name. Gina was weak, like…"

Leena. I stiffened. Cut off an angry retort.

"Leena, I'm not the carbon copy of Mom you think I am."

"I never thought of you as a carbon copy, Georgia. Me? I went straight for clone."

I laughed. She didn't

I snatched up the remote and flicked on the TV. "Let's watch the news." Anything to avoid talking.

After the inevitable fighting in the Middle East, politicians vying to outdo each other with half-truths, flooding in one place and wildfires in another came news closer to home.

"Our top story tonight: A thirty-two-year-old man was found beaten in a local park this morning. Details when we return."

As the first ad blared into the room, I hustled to the kitchen and opened the oven. A puff of steam burst out, carrying the tantalizing aroma of cheese, chicken and cream sauce. I closed the door and turned down the heat. After making a salad, I returned to the sofa and refilled our glasses. I sat down in time for the details of the top story.

"Emergency vehicles were called to the scene of a vicious beating early this morning. The thirty-two-year-old male victim was pronounced dead at the scene."

The camera highlighted a line of yellow police tape strung from one leafy tree to another. Beyond the tape, police officers milled about. An ambulance backed toward a tarp protecting what had to be the body, lying sadly alone beneath hanging branches that gave little protection from heavy rain.

"The victim's name has not been released pending notification of family. Police are asking anyone who was in the area of Centennial Park

before seven this morning to get in touch with them. Police are also searching for a woman who called 9-1-1 but fled the scene once paramedics arrived. She is described as being about five foot nine, with a slim athletic build, wearing shorts and a sweatshirt. She has shoulder-length, straight hair, possibly brown. Anyone who may have seen this woman is asked to contact police."

With a melodic bleep, the sound died and the screen went dark. Georgia dropped the remote to her lap. "Enough news," she said, her voice hoarse. She drained her wineglass and held it out with a shaky hand. "Fill 'er up."

* * *

The next morning, dressed for work in a jade-green blazer and black pencil skirt, I paused outside the tiny bedroom behind my kitchen. All was silent, so I tiptoed from the house, shut the door and got into my car. The night before, I'd told Georgia I worked in an office. I didn't mention it was a law office, didn't admit I was a legal assistant, couldn't stand to see her gloat. Seemed like all those summers Mom and Georgia had forced me to work in their law office paid off. Was that ironic or what?

The drive into our small island town takes fifteen minutes on a narrow, winding road. No traffic jams. Little traffic of any kind. My radio was tuned to the news, but I wasn't listening. Not until the name Branson jumped out at me. I turned up the volume.

"Police are searching for the victim's wife, Georgia Branson, as a person of interest. Ms. Branson's red suv was found at the airport this morning, but there is no sign of her. Anyone with information on her whereabouts is asked to call police."

I slammed on the brakes. Wheeled a one-eighty. Hit the gas.

FOUR

I stormed into my house, ready to drag Georgia out of bed. But her startled eyes met mine over the coffee machine.

"Coffee?" she asked, holding up the carafe I had brewed for her, thoughtful sister that I am. Then she smiled. "Just look at you, all dressed up like a lawyer."

I stared at her, speechless.

"Green suits you," she added. "It brings out the color of your eyes."

Did my sister just pay me a compliment, or was there more to come?

Georgia shrugged, replaced the carafe, picked up a blue pottery mug and limped to the table. She sat down with her back to me, her trusty nine iron across her lap. "Did you forget something?"

"No. But it seems you did."

The mug was halfway to her mouth. She lowered it abruptly. "I have no idea what you're talking about."

I marched to the far side of the table. Glared down at her. "You knew it was him, didn't you? You knew it was your husband."

Her brow furrowed. "What about Mark?"

"You knew it was his body they found in that park. That's why you shut off the TV last night."

Her face turned ashen. She stared at her ringless left hand, fingers around the mug. Her right hand gripped the nine iron like a club. "I...hoped it wasn't him. He ran there every morning."

I sank to the chair facing her. "Were you there?"

"What? Where? At the park? Why would you think that?"

"It's all over the news. The police are looking for you as a *person of interest*. And the description of the woman who fled the scene fits you almost perfectly. Except for your hair. Tell me, Georgia, did you cut it yourself? Because, you know, it couldn't look much worse."

"Thanks, little sister. You say the nicest things."

"You didn't answer my question."

"Okay. Whatever. I cut it yesterday in a Walmart restroom after I changed into my fancy new duds. Happy?"

"So you admit you're on the run."

"Maybe I am. But it's not what you think."

"Look, Georgia, I deserve an explanation. Because it seems to me that if I help you now, I can be charged with aiding a fugitive. You, being a high-priced lawyer, would know all about that, right?"

Her eyes—tawny lioness eyes—stared right through me. "It's a long story."

"Give me two minutes."

I called the office to say I couldn't come in that day. Family emergency. Then I poured myself a coffee. "Now we have all day."

"I thought he was trying to kill me," she whispered.

"So you decided to get him first, is that it?"

"Listen, uh—*Leena,* you've got to believe me. I didn't kill anyone."

"But you were there?"

"No. I have no idea who that woman was, but it wasn't me."

"So you're saying it's only a coincidence that she looked like you?"

"I'm saying it wasn't me. Would I call 9-1-1 and hang around if I'd killed him?"

Okay. Point one for Georgia. "So why are you on the run?"

"How was I supposed to know he was dead?" she screamed. Tears spilled down her cheeks. She wiped them away. "I ran for my life. Mark has so many friends—customers, business associates, guys in his car clubs, cops—I can't go anywhere without him knowing about it. That's why I changed my appearance." She ran her fingers through her mangled hair. "And ditched my car. There aren't many shiny red Porsche Cayennes around town."

"But why did you think he wanted to kill you?"

She hung her head. "It started last Thursday night. I worked late and was in the parkade, walking to my car, when I heard footsteps behind me. I stopped and turned around. A dark figure vanished into the shadows. I started walking faster. The footsteps followed, getting closer.

I broke into a run. The footsteps ran too. My car was a few feet away, and I had the key fob in my hand. I pressed the Panic button and the car started beeping and flashing.

"I realized my mistake when I couldn't hear the footsteps over the beeping. He got so close I felt his warm breath on my neck, smelled the Scotch he must have used to steady his nerves. I screamed.

"Just then a car squealed around the corner and screeched to a stop beside me, crammed with noisy teenaged boys. The driver's window opened. 'Hey, lady. Want a ride?' He waggled his eyebrows.

"'Did you see someone here?' I asked the kid.

"'You mean like that old guy taking off?'

"I turned and glimpsed a figure disappearing behind a post by the exit ramp. He wore a dark blue jogging suit—Mark has one just like it."

I nodded. What was there to say?

"The kids drove away. I jumped into my car, locked the doors and squealed out of there."

Georgia paused, blew her nose and carried on. "Two days ago he tried again. I was riding my bike on my usual route when a car screamed around the corner, coming right at me. I yanked my front wheel onto the curb and crashed on the sidewalk. The car scraped against a fire hydrant and was gone before I could move. It was a Volkswagen Beetle."

"Mark's car?"

"No. But he has a whole car lot to choose from."

"Did you see the driver?"

"I was busy being sprawled on the sidewalk."

"So that's a no."

She glared at me.

"Did you call the police?"

"Did you miss the part where I said some of his best friends are cops?"

"Then why wait two more days to take off?"

Georgia stood, limped to the sink and dumped out her coffee. She poured herself a fresh cup and leaned against the counter. "Early yesterday morning I was getting ready for work when I heard a noise downstairs. I grabbed this old nine iron I'd been keeping handy—first as a weapon, then doubling as a cane—and crept downstairs. The French doors in the kitchen were partway open. The door to the garage wasn't quite latched— they were both locked when I went to bed.

"Then I heard something in Mark's office and knew he was there. I headed straight for the garage, got in my car and drove away with nothing but my shoulder bag and golf club."

"Then you changed your appearance and left your car at the airport. But how did you get to the ferry terminal? And, come to think of it, how did you know where I was?"

"Oh, that." Georgia waved dismissively. "We've known where you were all along."

"But—"

"So there's a new walking path around the airport. I followed it and continued to the ferry terminal. It's not far—normally, I could do it easily. But with my gimpy leg I ended up hitching a ride most of the way."

"Georgia," I said quietly. "Mark was killed before dawn yesterday morning."

"Yes."

"Which means either someone else was in your house, or..."

"Or I'm lying to you."

I jumped up. "Lying or not, it won't take the police long to figure out you have a sister and track me down. And if someone else is out to get you, they can probably figure it out too."

I thought for a second. "Georgia, I know a guy who can hide you until I figure out what to do. Let's go."

FIVE

I tossed a few necessities into my backpack while Georgia shuffled about, borrowing toiletries and clothing she might need over the next days. In the car she pulled out a stack of hundred-dollar bills and peeled them off one at a time, handing them to me like playing cards.

"Don't look at me like that," she said. "You'll need money to get by. I have it."

"But—do you always carry this much cash on you?"

"I've been draining my bank accounts for two months," she said. "Just in case."

In case of what? I wanted to ask. But a glance at her face told me to shut up and drive.

* * *

My ancient car bounced up Vern's driveway through potholes the size of fishponds. Vern's front yard was, to put it mildly, not quite up to Georgia's standards. Waist-high weeds and brown grasses grew around and through rusted-out cars scattered here and there. Moss formed a lumpy green carpet on the roof of his rustic log cabin.

A wide porch hung crookedly across the front. Several of its boards were missing. The three stairs had long since rotted away and been replaced by a wide plank ramp. Vern waved and made his way down it. His hair was longer and wilder than I remembered, his full gray beard untamed. He wore leather sandals, ripped jeans and an untucked flannel shirt.

"What is he?" Georgia snarled. "A hippie wannabe?"

"No." I smiled and waved. "No, I'd say Vern is the real deal."

She grabbed my arm. "Leena, you cannot leave me here!"

"He's a good man, Georgia. I hitched a ride with Vern the day I left home. He brought me to the island. He gave me a place to stay until I found a job and a place of my own, and never asked for anything in return. But the important thing is that no one knows I know him. You'll be safe here."

"Right. If I don't die of some dread disease, with blood oozing from all my orifices."

I laughed. "It's not as bad as it looks."

"Good to know. Because, Leena, it looks appalling."

Vern invited us inside, which was surprisingly neat and clean. A tiny kitchen, a wall of books, comfy chairs set around a woodstove. There was a small bedroom at each end of the cabin. Looking around, Georgia appeared a little less tense.

"Did you disable your cell phone?" Vern asked her.

"Of course. I removed the battery after I called Leena."

"You called her? On your cell?" Vern turned to me.

"Georgia told me to take out my battery. And I always do what my big sister says."

She glared at me.

Vern pulled two cell phones from a kitchen drawer. He handed one to each of us. "Memorize the numbers," he said. "And use them to call each other. I'll give you my number too."

"Burner phones?"

"You got it." He grinned, revealing a missing front tooth. "No GPS. They come in handy in my line of work."

I'd never asked what Vern did for a living. Don't ask. Don't tell.

Within the hour I was bouncing back down his driveway. I glanced in my rearview mirror, expecting to see Georgia tottering after me waving her golf-club cane. But the driveway was empty. My stomach tightened. I was on a mission. My first case as a private-investigator wannabe. I needed to find out what really happened. Was someone trying to kill Georgia? The same person who killed Mark? Or did Georgia make that up to cover the fact that she'd murdered her own husband?

* * *

Sitting in my car on the open car deck of the ferry that serviced our small coastal island, I had a half hour to decide where to begin. I closed my eyes and went over the investigative techniques I had learned so far in my online courses.

By midafternoon I was still in my car, but staring at the windows of B&R Volkswagen. The first rule of any investigation is to start at the beginning. This is what I kept telling myself. The truth was, I had no clue whether this dealership was the beginning, the end or neither of the above. But I had to start somewhere, right?

I checked my hair and makeup in my visor mirror, took a deep breath and stepped out of the car. Aiming for a self-assured look, I tucked my handbag beneath my arm, held my head high and strode toward a wall of windows. But even in my trendy office attire, with my hair pulled back in a neat French braid, the reflection striding toward me looked a whole lot less confident than I had hoped. My step faltered. It wasn't too late. I could turn and walk away. No one would know.

Georgia was counting on me to prove her innocence. What if I learned otherwise?

What did I know of her marriage? I'd met Mark Branson exactly once, the day he and Georgia announced their engagement. Her perfect husband might have been a perfect jerk. He might have abused her. Might have been after her money. Might have…

Avoiding eye contact, I entered the showroom, taking in the bright openness, the metallic scent of new cars. I paused at a gleaming red convertible and rubbed my hand over its soft leather seat, trying to look interested. Hoping to blend in.

I needn't have bothered. No one noticed me. Salesmen clustered around the receptionist's desk, speaking in low tones. The young woman behind the desk dabbed at her eyes. Not surprising, given the recent news of Mark's death.

I strolled to the next car on display while casually scanning the names on office window panels. Mark Branson's at the end. Next to his, directly in front of me, Larry

Russell, sales manager. The man himself was seated behind his desk, staring at a computer screen. His hair was as thin and pale as his face. He wore narrow wire-rimmed glasses. His right elbow rested on his desk, his hand on his forehead. He glanced up, saw me watching him and motioned me into his office.

"Can I get you a coffee?" he offered.

Had he mistaken me for someone else? Someone important? I was about to decline when I realized I was on the verge of a caffeine emergency. The half cup I'd guzzled early that morning had long since worn off.

"Please," I said. "Black."

He leaned forward and pressed a button. "Two coffees please, Deedee. One black, one with cream."

He leaned back in his chair, his face glum. "As you can appreciate, this is a sad day for us, Miss...?"

I thought quickly. This man was Mark's business partner and friend. Chances were, he knew Mark's mother-in-law, Davida O'Neil. My mother. So I went for my father's last name, the name Mom refused to take, declaring it unsuitable for a lawyer. "Swindle," I told him. "Leena Swindle."

"Not the ideal name for an insurance adjuster, is it?" He snickered.

"Uh—no. So I'm glad I'm not one."

He tried not to look surprised.

"To be honest, I was driving into town to look at used vws when I heard one of the owners had been murdered. I was shocked when they said his name because I used to know Mark years ago. He was a really nice guy. I hear the police suspect his wife?"

Deedee arrived, bringing coffee. "It was her, all right. You should have heard her threaten him."

"Threaten?" I asked. "With what?"

"That's enough, Deedee," Larry said.

But the receptionist was too worked up to stop. "Georgia accused him of trying to run her down with that car he bought for his girlfriend."

Larry stood and ushered her out the door.

"Mark was cheating on his wife? That doesn't sound like the Mark I remember."

"If you ask me, he was a fool, cheating on a woman like Georgia."

"He told you this?"

"We all knew. He had the balls to sell that car right out from under our girl."

"Your girl?"

He smiled. "Deedee practically drooled over that little yellow Beetle from the moment it came in on trade." He glanced longingly after Deedee, then leaned toward me. "Don't tell her, but I'm this close to getting her another one." He curled one finger around another.

SIX

My first stakeout. While I never expected it to be the thrill of a lifetime, I was unprepared for such total, mind-numbing boredom. I yawned. My eyes watered. To pass the time, I reached into the side pocket of my shoulder bag and retrieved the notebook and pen I had purchased before coming here. Good old-fashioned pen and paper. Safe and easy to use. No batteries required. No embedded GPS chips.

I opened to the first page. Wrote the date at the top. Below that, in note form,

I jotted down the highlights of my interview with Larry Russell.

I turned the page. Wrote, *Waitress.* Below that, *Yellow Beetle.* Hearing a car approach, I looked up, and there it was. A cute little yellow Beetle headed straight for me. Now what do I do, I thought? Duck out of sight? Step out of my car? Clearly, I should have read the stakeout manual.

The little jellybean of a car nosed up to my bumper and jerked to a stop. Windshield glare made it impossible to see the driver, but I figured she could see me. So I grabbed the burn phone and pretended to talk.

The little car reversed and screeched into a parking space directly across from me. The sunshine-yellow door swung open and a young woman emerged. Early twenties, five eight or nine, she moved with the long-legged grace of an athlete. Her hair, tied in a ponytail, was a rich chestnut brown. From a distance and adding another seven years, this woman could be mistaken for Georgia. Before Georgia took shears to her own hair. The waitress ran into the restaurant as if she were late.

I grabbed my notebook. Next to *Waitress* I wrote, *Georgia look-alike, my age.* Beside *Yellow Beetle* I added, *Convertible, dark cloth top.* Then I tucked the notebook away, grabbed my keys and headed inside.

Closer to dinner than lunchtime, the restaurant was all but empty. A long-past-middle-aged couple ate in stony silence. Three men in business suits ignored each other, thumbs beating out text messages.

"For one?" A tiny girl who looked about twelve blinked up at me. Was that pity in her pale blue eyes? Who comes to a family restaurant alone?

"Yes," I said, waving my phone. "My friend bailed at the last minute."

Why did I feel the need to justify myself? Especially since, from the interest she showed, she wasn't even listening. She ushered me to a booth, brought coffee and a menu and vanished.

Five minutes later the waitress appeared. Her name tag read Christie. Close up, Christie didn't resemble Georgia so much, but still, in spite of having blue eyes, she could easily be mistaken for Georgia's sister. Unlike me. At five foot four, I like to think of myself as compact rather than short. With light brown hair, green eyes and a round face, I take after my father—or so I've been told. I scarcely remember the man. Good old Dad walked away when I was five, never to return. I have never forgiven him.

"Are you ready to order?" the waitress asked, her eyes red-rimmed and puffy.

"Yes. The shrimp wrap with Caesar salad, please." I handed her the menu.

"Perfect," she said.

Do they ever say you've made a bad choice?

"I'll grab you some more coffee."

When Christie returned, I was ready. "I'm looking to buy a used car. Do you know much about that dealership next door?"

In the act of pouring coffee, her hand wavered. "Shit." She stared at a brown pool around my coffee mug. "Let me grab a cloth."

I used the moment to rethink my strategy. Christie scurried back, her face pink.

"I'm sorry if I upset you," I said. "But to be honest, I went into that place earlier and no one seemed much interested in helping me. They were too busy standing around talking to each other. If it hadn't been for the sales manager—uh, Larry something— I would have walked out and never gone back. But then I heard one of the owners was murdered yesterday. I'm guessing you knew him?"

She studied her own hand wiping the table in a hypnotic, circular movement. "Mark used to come in here for lunch most days," she admitted. "I got to know him pretty well. He was a really nice guy. He didn't deserve what happened."

"His death must be upsetting for you," I said sympathetically.

She collapsed on the seat across from me. "You have no idea." She gulped, wiping away tears. She stood as abruptly as she had sat.

"As for buying a car from them…" Her eyes wandered in the direction of the dealership. "I don't know, I only dealt with Mark."

"You bought a car from him?"

She nodded. "A Beetle convertible."

"Oh, that cute little yellow one out there? I love it!"

She smiled, blinking back tears.

That's when I blew it. "Do you think his wife did it?" Which might have been okay if I hadn't added, "I heard he was having an affair."

Her face went blank. "I'll get some fresh coffee."

* * *

On the way back to my car, I wandered over to the yellow Beetle. Aiming for casual, I strolled around to the passenger side. And there it was. A bashed-in fender surrounded by red scrape lines. I glanced back toward the restaurant. Christie was watching me.

I grinned like an idiot, gave a thumbs-up, pointed to the dealership and scurried to my car.

SEVEN

I checked into the motel Georgia had recommended on the edge of town. It was reasonably new and reasonably quiet, and my room was clean—no bedbugs. I checked. Nothing spectacular, the room contained the usual queen-sized bed, a bureau with mirror, a desk, two armchairs, a miniature table and a TV. I changed into jeans, a red hoodie and sneakers, hung my office duds on a rack outside the bathroom and placed my pumps below. My T-shirts and lingerie went in a drawer, and I was done.

Settling on the bed, I pulled out Vern's burn phone and dialed Georgia's number.

She answered in seconds. "Colleen?"

"It's *Leena*, not Colleen. Can't you remember that?" I spat her words back at her. *Tell me again why I'm helping this woman?* I took a deep breath and started again. "I'm at the motel and need to ask you a few questions."

"Such as?"

"You never said what color of Beetle ran you off the road."

"The most gaudy yellow you can imagine. Like a bad weed."

"As opposed to a good weed?"

"What?"

"Nothing. So a yellow Volkswagen Beetle. Anything else?"

"Uh—yes. It was a convertible with the top up. Dark cloth, I think."

"Interesting."

"Why? Did you see it on the lot?"

"What? No. I'm just following a lead, Georgia."

"Well, listen to you. Talking like a real detective. Just like you always wanted."

I squeezed my eyes shut. I would not let her get to me.

"And?" she asked.

"And what?"

She made an impatient sound in her throat "You had *a few* questions."

"Right. What happens to Mark's half of the dealership with him gone?"

"Gone? Mark isn't gone, *Leena,* not like our ne'er-do-well father. He's dead. Dead," she repeated, her voice hard.

I couldn't think how to reply. Couldn't decide if she was angry, hurting or both.

She drew a quick breath. "Mark didn't own half. He owned a one-third share. Larry owns one third. The final third is

55

mine because of the loan I made to help them get started." Her voice broke.

I waited.

"If Mark had divorced me, I would have demanded my money back immediately."

"Yes, you mentioned that before. So divorce wouldn't be a good business move on his part. But your share is still yours with him dead, right?"

"Of course. In a divorce, if he couldn't pay up I would have taken over his share as well as keeping mine."

"Harsh." But a perfect motive for Mark to murder Georgia rather than divorce her.

"But we also signed a partnership agreement for the dealership. In the event one partner dies, the remaining two split his share of the business."

"So you and Larry each own half now."

"Right." Georgia sounded as if she couldn't care less. "Mark and Larry took out life insurance on all the money they borrowed."

"Which means you get your money back and own half of a profitable car dealership free and clear?" An excellent reason for Georgia to murder her husband.

"Leena," Georgia broke into my thoughts, "I'd like to know if Mark changed his will. We each left *all our worldly goods* to the other. I changed my will the day he moved out, leaving my half of everything we owned to Mom. But life's little details never mattered much to Mark."

So, I wondered, how many new widows focus in on the money so soon after their loss? But then I reminded myself that Mark and Georgia had separated. That made a huge difference. And Georgia was, first and foremost, a lawyer. Legal details gave meaning to her life.

"Georgia, did O'Neil and Branson write your wills?"

"We did. But naturally Mark would hire another law firm to change it."

Did I hear a sob? Real? Faked? Lawyer-style dramatics? I gave her the benefit of my doubt. "Listen, Georgia, I'm sorry, but I need to ask one more question. If Mark did change his will, could he have made his girlfriend the beneficiary?"

"What? The bimbo? Get half my house? If he tried that I'd kill him!"

"Uh…Georgia?"

She gasped. "I didn't mean that."

"If not to the girlfriend, who?"

"His precious little Porsche Boxster, for all I know," she snapped.

"Mark drove a Porsche too? Shouldn't you both be driving Volkswagens?"

She sighed. "We do, sort of, since Porsche is part of the Volkswagen Group. Mark always loved zipping around in sports cars, but I'm more the practical type. Hence the suv."

Made you wonder what they had in common.

"Listen, Leena, I need you to check Mark's safe in his office at home. If his will is gone, we'll know he made a new one."

Okay. Georgia's concern over the will might make me uncomfortable, but I now had the perfect excuse to check out her house and confirm her story of a break-in. Before I'd left the island, Georgia had given me her keys. Now she gave me the combination to Mark's safe.

Outside the motel streetlights were on, darkness creeping in. I decided to save Georgia's little task for the next day and instead walked to a convenience store a block from the motel.

I returned with a bag of chocolate-chip cookies, a package of carrot muffins, some bananas and a six-pack of raspberry yogurt that I placed in the tiny refrigerator in my room. Then I sat at the desk and went over my notes, adding a new thought here and there. Before bed I sipped tea and munched cookies along with yogurt and banana while watching the news. There was nothing about Mark's murder. The media had moved on.

* * *

My first break and enter. Okay, not technically a *break*, since I used a key, but it was definitely an *enter* and probably illegal thanks to the yellow police tape wrapped around the exterior. *Crime Scene. Do Not Enter.*

I glanced around. No one here. No police cars in sight. No neighbors' noses pressed to their windows. I ducked under the tape and entered, heart pounding.

The massive foyer soared up two stories to a vaulted ceiling. A grand staircase swept off to the right. The hardwood floor gleamed under daylight from windows high on the second floor. I wondered who had to wash them.

If I were into that sort of thing, I'd be able to identify the expensive-looking area rug in the center of the foyer, the delicate vase displayed on an ornate table and the pedigree of the table itself. But I wasn't so I couldn't. Carrying my sneakers, my bag slung over my shoulder, I tiptoed across a huge expanse of floor and down the wide hallway. I haven't a clue why I tiptoed, except that the house was so quiet, so churchlike, I didn't want to disturb a thing.

I followed Georgia's directions to Mark's office. Dark wood desk, black leather chair, picture window overlooking a perfectly manicured back lawn. I found the safe behind his desk, hidden by an abstract painting. How predictable is that? I opened it no problem, pulled out a stack of papers and found the will. I stuffed it in my shoulder bag and put everything else back. Then I went to the kitchen.

Georgia had said the French doors were partially open. They were closed now, locked and bolted. I opened them, ducked under yellow tape and stepped out to examine the lock from both sides. No sign of forced entry. The patio consisted of interlocking cement blocks sculpted around a flowerbed. Two dirty footprints led from the flowerbed to the doors. There were deep footprints in the soil of the flowerbed.

Did that mean something? Possibly. It had rained the morning Mark was killed, meaning a muddy garden. But if someone had entered her house, as Georgia said, why walk through the dirt first? Unless to peek through the closed blinds of the window behind the breakfast nook?

I inserted the battery in my smart-phone, placed my sneakers beside the footprints, snapped photos and removed the battery again. Back inside, something had changed. The churchlike quiet was gone. Footsteps clomped across the foyer. No attempt at quiet.

EIGHT

"**W**hat are you doing here?"

The young cop who appeared in the doorway was so fresh-faced his uniform looked like a Halloween costume. One hand hovered over his gun belt, the other clutched a Tim Hortons coffee cup. A circle of donut sugar on his lips did nothing to enhance the scary-policeman look he was going for.

The words *the best defense is a good offense* popped into my head. So I pulled myself up to my full five four and glared back at him. "I have a right to be here. What's your excuse for barging in like this?"

He sauntered into the kitchen. "Didn't you see the police tape? It's my job to make sure no one breaks in."

"That's very considerate of you. Georgia would be pleased. But if you mean me, I didn't break in—I happen to have a key."

"I could arrest you for trespassing." He placed his coffee on the granite countertop, crossed his arms and set his feet wide apart.

If his stance was meant to intimidate me, it wasn't working. "Will you please explain how I can be trespassing in my own sister's home?"

"No one mentioned a sister."

"I'm not surprised. We haven't spoken in three years." As soon as the words slipped out, I realized my mistake. When I'd left home, Georgia was engaged to Mark and they had yet to purchase this house. Would this boy-cop know that? I hoped not.

"But when I heard Georgia was missing, I came straight here, hoping to find something, some clue as to where she may have gone. I'm worried about her."

He picked up his coffee. A man of few words.

"Why put tape around her house anyway? This isn't a crime scene."

"We're searching for evidence."

"Evidence of what? And exactly who is doing the searching? Because I don't see anyone."

"We're mostly done," he admitted. "But you can't be too careful in a murder investigation."

"Murder? But Mark was killed in a park, not here." I gasped. Slapped a hand over my mouth, every bit as melodramatic as my sister—maybe I would make a good lawyer after all. "Oh my god! Please tell me it wasn't a murder-suicide!" I swayed as if about to faint. "You found her body upstairs, didn't you?"

He put down his coffee again and gripped my upper arms. "Calm down, ma'am. Your sister might be a murderer, but she's very much alive."

"You found her?"

"Not yet."

"Then how can you know she's alive?" I pushed away from him. "Wait—you think my sister murdered her husband?" I shook my head. "That's impossible. Georgia would never hurt anyone."

He tucked his thumbs into his belt. "Then how do you explain the murder weapon we found in the back of that fancy SUV of hers?"

This time I really did feel faint. I put a hand on the countertop to steady myself. The cold granite sent a chill through my body.

His face froze. He stepped closer. "Look, I didn't mean…forget I said that, uh, Ms.…?"

"Leena…um…Leena O'Neil." I offered my hand. "And you are?"

"Constable Ryan Pinnelli."

We shook hands like new friends, as if we might grow to like each other one day. "Don't worry, Constable Pinnelli, I'll keep your little secret so long as you promise not to tell anyone I was here. I want to find my sister, and I intend to prove she didn't murder anyone."

He snickered.

"Something funny?"

"Look, Ms. O'Neil…"

"Call me Leena. It feels more like me."

"Leena, you should leave the police work to us. We're the professionals. You'll only get yourself in trouble."

"You're telling me police never make a mistake? Never arrest the wrong person? Never shoot first and ask questions later?"

His eyes hardened. His face turned pink. "I'm saying we know what we're doing."

"What if I tell you I'm studying criminology and investigative strategies? I'm practically a private investigator and highly trained in finding missing persons."

Again the snicker, the shaking of his head. "So you took Criminology 101 online and think that qualifies you for police work?"

Ouch.

He placed a hand under my elbow. "You need to get out of here before my partner gets back. He won't let you off so easy."

"Tell me what the murder weapon was and I'll be out of here."

"I have no idea what you're talking about." He marched me to the front door and pulled it open.

I ducked under the yellow tape in time to see a police car round the corner.

"Ms. O'Neil," Pinnelli said, his voice formal, "I'll need your phone number in case we have questions for you."

I hesitated. Which number should I give him? Could the police have traced those first calls between my phone and Georgia's? To be safe, I gave him the burn phone number. Pinnelli handed me a business card. "Call us if you hear from your sister," he said.

"Will do."

The cop car pulled into the driveway as I reached the bottom stair. I glanced back at Constable Pinnelli. "You might want to lick your lips before he gets here," I suggested.

I could feel the eyes of Pinnelli's partner following me as I scurried to my car.

"Who the hell is that?" he yelled before I slammed my door.

NINE

Leaving my sister's neighborhood, I watched for a place to pull over. One where I wouldn't be noticed if Pinnelli's partner decided to follow. I wheeled into a small strip mall, drove past rows of empty parking spaces and squeezed between an SUV and a minivan. Then I called Georgia.

"Care to explain how the murder weapon got in your car?"

She remained silent for so long I thought we had been disconnected. "Georgia?"

"Excuse me?" She sounded more annoyed than surprised.

"The weapon that killed your husband was found in your car," I said. "By the police."

"And you know this how?"

"I'm not at liberty to say."

"Oh, *please.* What are you, Homeland Security? Next you'll be telling me it's on a need-to-know basis." She paused for a quick breath. "What is it?"

"What is what?"

She groaned. "The murder weapon, *Leena,* what is it?"

"You tell me."

"How can I tell you when I have no idea? Listen, I left the house with my shoulder bag and the nine iron I've kept with me since that first attempt on my life. As you know, I brought it with me to the island. And, before you ask, I did not club my husband to death with it."

"Georgia, you're not listening to me. Of course your nine iron isn't the murder weapon. Want to know why? *Because the police found the murder weapon in your car!*"

"That's simply not possible."

"What was in your car?"

"I don't know...nothing."

"Think, Georgia. Something in the back? Something sturdy enough to beat a man to death, like a tire iron?" Even saying these words sent a shudder through me.

Georgia too, judging by the tremor in her voice. "My brand-new set of clubs was in the back, under the privacy panel. I haven't had a chance to try them out yet."

"Do you lock your car every time you park it?"

"Always, even in my own garage."

"Who else has keys to your car?"

"Mark...uh...no one."

I heard the catch in her voice, and my heart gave a little twist. This must be so difficult for her. Unless it was all an act.

* * *

Georgia told me exactly where her run-in with the VW had occurred, as I wanted to take a look for myself. But it had happened in an area of the city I wasn't familiar with. I had never invested in GPS, so I yanked out a stack of papers from my glove box and leafed through them until I found a city map. Then I traced out the fastest route.

The route took me right past the VW dealership. Georgia's words flashed through my mind as I drew near. *He has a whole car lot to choose from.* I turned onto the lot. From the customer parking area I could see Larry standing in his office, his phone to his ear. Moments later he hung up, spoke briefly to Deedee and strode out a side door. I ducked when he climbed into a silver Jetta and drove past me. Then I went inside.

"Can I help you?" A blond woman, mid-thirties, wearing a business suit and low-heeled pumps, appeared out of nowhere.

"Uh, yes, I hope so. I'm interested in buying a used car."

"Then you're in luck." She looked me up and down, from my red hoodie to my jeans and gray sneakers. "We happen to have a good selection of inexpensive used vehicles right now. Mint condition, low mileage, practically a steal."

"All of them?" I asked, but she wasn't listening.

She hustled me out the side door. "They're at the back of the lot," she said. "Let's go take a look, and if one catches your eye we can do a test drive."

"Sounds good to me."

She touched my arm as if we were old friends. "I'm Fiona, and you are?"

"Uh, Leena."

There were rows of small and midsize cars that all looked pretty much the same to me. Fiona zeroed in on a pale brown one I instantly disliked. "This is the perfect vehicle for a young woman like yourself."

"You mean boring?"

Her eyes widened, but she moved on.

Half an hour later I had sat in too many cars to keep track, put the seats back and forward, looked through the windshields, studied the engines and asked several dozen stupid questions. All the while Fiona pelted me with facts and figures I instantly forgot.

"How about taking it for a test drive?" she asked, not for the first time.

I climbed out of the current vehicle, something small and blue. "I don't think so," I said, also not for the first time. "To tell you the truth, Fiona, none of these cars turn me on. But you know, I've always liked those little Beetles, especially the convertibles. I don't suppose you happen to have any?"

She stared at me. Surprised? Confused? Angry? Wondering why I didn't say this in the first place?

"I'll need to check," she said, "but it seems to me one came in on trade last week." She started back toward the building.

I trotted after her. "If you have one, I'll take it for a test drive. Especially if it happens to be yellow—my favorite color."

"Then let's hope it is!"

So. The plot thickened. Maybe Georgia was right. Maybe Mark really had been out to kill her, using a car that could be mistaken for Christie's. But why go to all that trouble? If he wanted to implicate Christie, why not simply borrow her car? And why would he want to implicate his girlfriend anyway? Unless he hadn't liked Christie as much as Georgia believed.

If Mark really had tried to run her down, that still did not clear Georgia of his murder—far from it. Could be, realizing he was out to get her, she decided to beat him to it—no pun intended.

Fiona left me standing alone in the showroom. I tried to blend in, tried not to look out of place, although I knew I did. I wandered over to a rack of brochures. Picked up one and studied the pictures as if about to splurge on a brand-new vehicle.

I used this time to consider the huge, gaping hole in my theory. If Mark had tried to run Georgia over with a car from his lot and not with Christie's car, why was there damage to her fender? Coincidence? Even for me that was a bit too much to believe. So, if it was Christie's Beetle that ran Georgia off the road, why was I wasting my time here? One of them must have done it. Either Mark or Christie. They both had ample motive. I put the brochure back and turned to go.

"Great news!" Fiona said, her voice echoing about the cavernous room. "We have one used Beetle convertible. It's in the shop right now, and get this—it's your favorite color, yellow!"

Where Larry came from I still don't know. It was like they did some magic thing with mirrors in that place, the way salespeople appeared without warning. Anyway, the next thing I knew he was standing beside me.

"Ah! Ms. Swindle, back so soon. Are you still looking for a car?"

"Uh, yes. I don't have much time, so I came back to have a look."

"I see." He turned to the saleswoman. "Thank you, Fiona, I'll take it from here. Since we aren't busy, why don't you take your lunch break now?"

She stared at him with a mix of surprise and annoyance. Then she scowled at me and stomped away.

I watched her go, feeling guilty, although I wasn't sure why.

TEN

"**D**on't feel bad," Larry said, as if reading my mind. "Fiona thinks she'll miss out on her commission if you purchase a vehicle from me. But in that event, I would share it with her, naturally."

I wasn't sure how to answer this, considering I had no intention of buying a car. "I don't think I'm interested in a car that's been damaged," I said.

His head snapped toward me. "Damaged? Who told you that?"

"No one. Fiona said it was in the shop, so I assumed there was a problem with it."

"Then you assumed wrong. Our mechanics go through every vehicle that comes in on trade to be sure they're in perfect condition. After that they're detailed in the body shop until they look as good as new."

"All right, then. May I have a look at it?"

"I'm afraid we don't allow customers in the shop due to safety concerns."

"Just a peek, then? Through the door?"

"Sorry, but no." He gestured toward the exit and fell into step beside me. "I'll tell you what though. If you give me your phone number, I'll call you in a couple of days to arrange a test drive. How does that sound?"

I gave him the number of the burner phone. "Promise you won't sell it to Deedee in the meantime?"

"The customer always comes first," he said. Taking my arm, he ushered me out the door.

I settled behind my steering wheel. Watching. Larry scuttled to his office and sat down out of sight.

If I couldn't see him, he couldn't see me. Even so, to be on the safe side I started my car and drove around the building to the shop entrance rather than walking there. I parked and went to the door, where I tried to see through a dirty square of glass. No luck. So I pushed open the door and came face to face with a man built like a vending machine in orange coveralls.

He smiled politely. "I'm sorry, ma'am, but customers aren't permitted in this area."

"Oh, but I was told you had a yellow Beetle in here? That's exactly the car I've been looking for, so I was hoping to take a quick look."

I craned my neck to see around the breadth of him. He stepped closer, reached around me and opened the door. "I suggest you speak with a salesperson," he said.

For the third time that day, I got kicked out by a man. This was not good for the ego.

I consulted my map and continued to the scene of Georgia's accident. It was in a residential area near the intersection of two quiet backstreets. I spotted the fire hydrant, pulled over and got out. There wasn't much to see. No broken glass, no skid marks, no tire tracks on the strip of grass around the hydrant. Nothing out of the ordinary.

Nothing but traces of yellow on the red paint of the hydrant. I assembled my phone, snapped a half dozen photos and removed the battery again. Then I set off to find an electronics store. There was something I needed to buy.

* * *

It was late afternoon when I turned into the lot of Jamie's Family Restaurant. I was in luck. Christie's yellow Beetle was there, and the space next to it, on the passenger side, was vacant. I backed in. The red scrapes were glaringly obvious. This little car had tried to run down my sister. But who was behind the wheel?

Reassembling my phone, I rolled down my window, took photos of the fender, then sat back, breathing as heavily as if I had just run five miles. I glanced toward the restaurant windows but couldn't see anything from this angle. I hoped no one was watching as I climbed out, sidled to the front of Christie's car and snapped photos showing both the fender and the license plate. My phone was still in my hand when a soft footstep made me whirl around. Christie. She didn't look happy.

Growing up, I'd had plenty of practice making up believable stories. Every time I messed up, which was more often than I care to admit, either my mother or her little clone, Gina, would grill me. The result? I had become an accomplished liar who could think on her feet. A valuable trait in my new line of work.

Rule number one. Be aggressive. I stepped toward her, slipping my phone into my pocket. "Oh, it's you—Christie, isn't it?"

She studied my face, as if trying to place me.

"I'm Leena. Remember I was in yesterday and we talked?"

"Oh, right. Shrimp wrap and Caesar."

I smiled. "It was good too."

Her eyes remained on my face, waiting for an explanation. Approaching from behind and partially blocked by my old clunker of a car, Christie may or may not have seen me take the photos. But she had definitely caught me looking at her car.

"So anyway, as I said before, I love these little Beetles, and yellow is my favorite color. My car's a wreck, as you can see." I gestured toward the old heap, looming dark and sinister beside the cheery little

Beetle. "And it turns out they have one just like this next door, but it's in the shop and they wouldn't let me see it. So I came back to take a closer look at yours. I hope you don't mind?"

I was babbling, I knew. Too much information is the number-one sign you're lying.

"Did you take a photo?" She eyed me warily. "What's going on?"

This woman asked too many questions. Making up neat little lies for my mother had never taken much effort, because she always lost interest before I was halfway through my story.

"So, okay, here's the deal. I'm new in town and looking for a job. I've worked in restaurants before, and this seems like a great place to work—with friendly staff and all—so I decided to come back. When you caught me standing here looking at your car, I was trying to work up the nerve to go inside. So—do you know if they're hiring?"

"Uh, I'm not sure. But we have been getting busier recently, so maybe. Did you bring a résumé?"

"Actually, no. But I can drop one off tomorrow if you think it's worth the effort."

She put a hand to her forehead. "Sure, whatever. My manager should be in by eleven. Why don't you come back then?" As she moved past me to the driver's side, her eyes swept across her right front fender.

"I couldn't help noticing the damage," I said. "What happened?"

"Damned if I know. I noticed it a few days back, after..." Her voice broke. She pressed her fingers over her mouth. "Sorry...I noticed it the same day I found out about my—uh—about Mark Branson. Some jerk must have sideswiped it when I was working the night before."

"Did you call the cops?"

"Sure, but what are they going to do? They didn't even bother showing up—they said to call my insurance company and be done with it." Christie wiped tears from under her eyes.

First impressions may be lasting, but they aren't always right. I knew that. Christie could be as skilled a liar as I liked to believe I was. Even so, I liked her and felt sorry for her at the same time. I needed to know more.

"Hey, it looks like you could use a drink. What do you say?"

She looked hesitant.

"Listen, Christie, I just arrived in town and I'm staying in a motel. I don't know a soul here and have nothing to do this evening. I guess what I'm saying is, I could use some company and right now you look like you could use a friend. So if you're okay with that, tell me where to meet. I'm buying."

ELEVEN

The pub perched on the edge of the sea. Inside, it was all glass and wood, with a vaulted ceiling and small tables scattered around a circular gas fireplace. Classy. There were few patrons so early in the evening. We chose a table for two overlooking the water. The sea was darkening, but sunlight still lingered on jagged mountain peaks across the strait.

We each ordered a glass of red wine. Sitting face to face, I couldn't think how to begin. In my mind I listed everything I needed to know. But how do you casually ask someone if she tried to run over her boyfriend's wife with her car? Or if he borrowed her car that day to do the deed himself?

Our drinks arrived. "Cheers!" Red wine trickled down my throat, warm and soothing. "This tastes like more."

Christie gulped at hers. "We should have ordered a carafe."

"It's not too late. Carafe soon. Cab later."

She laughed.

Quiet music played in the background, and the sea below us turned deep blue. "My boyfriend dumped me," I said, surprising myself. Now that I'd said it, I had no choice but to elaborate. "We lived together for two years," I added. "He wanted out, but the house was his, so it was me who had to leave."

"Bummer. You should go after him for half."

"Yeah, like that's going to happen. But to be honest, it wasn't all bad. He gave back most of the money I paid him to help with his mortgage, so I'm good for a while."

"Men are bums." She chugalugged the remainder of her wine.

"I'll drink to that." I took a small sip, determined to limit my intake. With another glass or two in her, Christie would tell all.

"Hey, looks like your drink evaporated," I said. "Time for that carafe!"

When it arrived, I refilled her glass.

"What about yours?"

"I'll finish this first," I said. "I don't want to mix my wines."

She downed it and plunked her glass down. She stared into her wineglass. "My boyfriend dumped me too."

My jaw dropped. Literally. I pushed it back up. "Really? Want to talk about it?"

"No." She turned the glass slowly, not looking up. "He's dead," she whispered.

"What?"

"Clubbed to death with a golf club." She looked at me.

Tears streamed down her face. "We met in the park, like every morning. That was our thing, you know? A run together before work. But that morning he gave me the old line. *It's been fun, but it's over. Think I'll go on back to the wife now.*"

"His wife?" I exclaimed. This changed everything. If Mark really was going back to Georgia, had she lied by saying she didn't believe him? But Christie was staring at me. I lowered my voice. "He was married?"

"Separated. But the jerk still loved her and wanted to go back. *If she'll have me,* he said. He said he needed to break up with me first, to prove he meant what he said."

"Wait a minute. You're talking about Mark Branson, aren't you? From the Volkswagen dealership? You're the other woman! You're the witness who disappeared."

She nodded, blubbering.

"So...what? You beat him to death because he dumped you?"

She looked horrified. "What? No! I could never hurt Mark."

"You loved him?"

"I liked him a lot, and we had fun together, but it wasn't a forever kind of thing." She wiped her eyes, blew her nose and pushed her wineglass away. "I need a coffee."

When the server brought two black coffees, we ordered a plate of red-hot chicken wings and another of fried zucchini sticks. We didn't speak again until the food sat in front of us.

"You must have been angry when he broke up with you."

"Damn right! I mean, first he leaves his wife for me, and then he changes his mind. Who does that?"

"I felt like clobbering my ex too."

"Okay, sure, I killed him, all right. I clobbered him with the golf club I just happened to take with me that day." She grabbed a chicken wing. "The truth is, he felt bad. He even sweetened the breakup by promising to pay for my car. That's not going to happen now—so why would I kill him?"

Why indeed? Unlike Georgia, Christie had nothing to gain. "Tell me what you saw."

She put down her coffee. "What's with all the questions? What are you, a cop?"

"Listen, Christie, to be totally honest, I'm a private investigator." Okay, maybe not *totally* honest, but close enough.

"Seriously? Who are you working for?"

"I'm sorry, that's confidential."

"If you tell me you gotta kill me, right?"

I laughed. "My client doesn't believe the wife is guilty. The client says police never have enough time or money to do a thorough investigation."

"So you're a real PI? Like Kinsey Millhone?"

"Except that Kinsey is fictional. Don't tell me you read Sue Grafton too?"

"I started reading her mysteries when I was twelve. I've read every one so far. I wanted to be a private detective too, but my parents insisted I go into accounting, like them. So I compromised. I'm taking forensic accounting at college."

"Whoa—you're like the sister I never had!"

"I'll drink to that." Christie raised her coffee cup.

"True confession," I said. "This is my first case, and I'm scared of messing up." I pulled my newly acquired mini-recorder from my bag and placed it on the table between us. "Could you please tell me exactly what happened?"

Christie stared at the device, smaller than a cell phone.

"You owe him the truth, right? Tell me what happened after he broke it off."

"I told him to go to hell and he took off down the path. I started for home. He yelled and I turned back in time to catch a flash of metal above the bushes, reflected from a streetlight behind me. I'm almost sure it was a golf club. It went down. There was this loud—sickening—thud." She shuddered.

"I screamed. The bushes rustled and someone ran away, head and shoulders over the bushes, wearing a dark hoodie. That's all I saw in the rain and dim light. I found Mark lying on the ground—blood everywhere! So I called 9-1-1 and stayed with him until the paramedics came, then took off. Don't ask me why. Force of habit, I guess. I got so used to sneaking around to hide our affair, I didn't know how to quit."

"Christie, trust me, I'm going to catch whoever did this. But do you really think it was his wife?"

She counted on her fingers. "She knew he ran there every morning. Dead pays better than divorce. Oh, and the clincher? Georgia plays golf."

"Can you think of anyone else who might have wanted him out of the way?"

She shook her head. "Mark was a great guy. Everyone liked him."

I turned off the mini-recorder. We chatted for a while about anything but Mark and murder. The carafe sat almost untouched. Seemed like a waste, but there you go. At least we wouldn't need to pay for taxis.

"It was good having someone to talk to," she said as we left. "Let's exchange phone numbers and maybe do this again sometime."

"Good idea." I reached for the burn phone in my purse.

"It's in your pocket," she said.

"What?"

"You put your phone in your pocket when I came out of the restaurant. It's still there—I can see it."

"Oh, right." So I gave her my smartphone number instead.

TWELVE

Back at the motel, I emailed the photos from my phone to my home computer as a backup. Then I replayed my recording from the pub. Christie's words came through loud and clear. I listened twice, making notes, then read through my notebook, trying to make sense of it all. No matter how I interpreted the evidence, one thing was for sure. It wasn't looking good for my sister.

Questions. If the murder weapon was a golf club, was it Georgia's? Was it from her new set? If she was innocent, how did the club end up in her car?

Georgia had both motive and opportunity. Christie thought Georgia killed him out of jealousy and greed. She didn't know Georgia had a third, more powerful motive. Her husband was trying to kill her.

Or did she? What if Mark and Christie were in on it together? What if Mark was the man in the parkade? He failed, so Christie, angry, went after Georgia with her car.

Georgia insisted someone had been in her house early on the morning of the murder. Obviously, it could not have been Mark, who was quite dead. Or Christie, who was still with him at the park.

So either Christie or Georgia was lying. Sadly, I wanted to believe them both. Georgia, because she was my sister. Christie, because I liked her.

Now what? If I were a real private investigator, would I know what to do next?

I sat back, took a deep breath. What does any good detective really need? Common sense, persistence and an eye for detail. A mystery is like a giant jigsaw puzzle. Gather all the pieces, fit them together, and you'll see the whole picture. But how do you know when you have all the pieces?

I hadn't made notes about my visit to Georgia's house, but now I took a close look at the photos. The footprints were clear enough, and they helped back up Georgia's story, but they were small for a man and large for a woman. As evidence, they meant nothing.

The murder weapon in her vehicle was damning. Except that only a fool would commit murder and drive around with the weapon behind her backseat. And Georgia was no fool.

Then I remembered the will. I pulled it from my bag and skimmed through it. Mark left everything he owned to Georgia, including half of his share of the dealership, just as Georgia said. But if Mark had changed his will, could he have left that half share to someone else? Christie?

I had no way of knowing. The fact that Mark had not taken the will from his safe didn't prove anything. He could have hired a lawyer to write a new one. And that new one, if it existed, might provide Christie with ample motive to do him in.

I lay awake for hours trying to fit the pieces together. When at last I drifted into a restless sleep, I dreamed of Volkswagen Beetles. Dozens of them. All yellow, all with a damaged front fender. My eyes popped open. The room was dark and still. The answer felt as close as my dream. But like a dream, it slipped away.

The next time I awoke the room was bright, the morning half gone. I rolled out of bed, made coffee in the motel's little machine and padded to the bathroom for a shower.

The coffee wasn't half bad. I guzzled a cup, swallowed a two-day-old carrot muffin and read my notes one more time. One thing bugged me. Not a missing piece but an extra piece. And I had no clue what to do with it.

I grabbed the burn phone and called Georgia.

"Please tell me I can get out of here today!" she wailed. No hello. No "how are you?" Georgia never wasted time on small talk.

I followed suit. "Why didn't you tell me Mark was coming back to you?"

That shut her up.

"Georgia? He dumped Christie because he was still in love with you."

"I didn't know. I swear."

"And if you had?" *If you had known, would you have killed him?* I wanted to ask, but the words stuck in my throat. You don't accuse your sister of murder and expect her to forgive you. Ever.

"You mean, would I have taken him back?"

"Uh—would you?"

"I don't know, Leena." Her words sounded like a sob. "Probably…"

"You could have forgiven him?"

"You think I'm pathetic, don't you?"

"Not at all, Georgia. I think you loved him and he hurt you." I thought for a moment. "But tell me, do you take your SUV to B&R Volkswagen for servicing?"

"Sure, it's free there. But what's that got to do with anything?"

"When was the last time you took it in?"

"Mmm…I think…a couple of weeks ago. I left it for the day. Why?"

"And you left your keys with it?"

"How else would they move it into the garage?"

How indeed?

* * *

After talking to Georgia, I had more questions for Christie. And a perfect excuse to stop by the restaurant, since it was Christie who'd suggested I bring in a résumé. I didn't have a printer, so I chose the old pen-and-paper method to create a suitable résumé.

"Skills and Experience" required some creative techniques. So. I've eaten in a lot of restaurants over the years. I worked at McDonald's during high school. All valuable restaurant experience, right? My next step was to find the nearest Staples, print it out and make copies.

By the time I entered Jamie's Family Restaurant, armed with a small stack of résumés in a new manila folder, the place was bustling with a noisy lunch crowd. A young server hurried up to me, menus in hand.

"Is Christie in today?" I asked.

"Um—I think she's on late shift. Table for one?"

"Actually, no. Christie said you might be hiring. I was hoping to talk to the manager?" I patted my résumé folder.

"Um, we're kinda busy right now. Maybe you could come back later?"

"Sure, great idea. Thanks." My hand was reaching for the door when I saw them. Four men in dark suits, approaching fast. In the lead was Larry Russell. I turned away.

"Want me to take your résumé for you?" the server asked.

"Thanks. No. I'll be back. Mind if I use the restroom?" I didn't wait for her reply.

THIRTEEN

Ten minutes later I slinked from the restroom and out the restaurant door. I walked past my car to the sidewalk. It bordered the busiest street in the city and took me back to the VW dealership.

At first the showroom seemed empty. No salesmen waiting to pounce on the first unsuspecting customer who wandered through the double doors.

"Hi there," a female voice called. "Are you looking for Larry?"

Deedee was watching me over the low wall that separated her desk from the main showroom.

"Uh, sure, if he's here. Or Fiona—she was very helpful yesterday."

"Let me see. Larry's at a lunch meeting. Fiona is somewhere on the lot. Can I page her for you?"

"That'd be great. Thanks."

A few minutes later Fiona stepped inside with a wide smile on her face. It vanished when she saw me. "Hello," she said. "Leena, isn't it?"

"Yes. And I'm sorry about what happened yesterday. You spent a lot of time with me, and I appreciate that. I didn't know Larry would come along. But he said if I buy from him he'll split the commission with you."

"Really." She didn't look impressed.

"I used to work in car sales," I said, wondering where I was going with this.

She looked surprised.

"But I found it scary not knowing what my paycheck would be every month."

"That's so true."

"Of course, there were perks," I added. "Like choosing any used car to drive home at night. Do you get to do that?"

She brightened. "Yes, any salesperson can take a car home. We just need to sign for it."

"Cool. Deedee too? And the owners?"

"It only applies to sales staff, so we can familiarize ourselves with the cars. But the owners can drive off in any vehicle they want and never sign anything."

"Lucky them! Do they do that often?"

"Yeah, I don't know. Larry does. Mark doesn't, er...didn't. He loved that little sports car of his." Her eyes teared up. "I'm sorry, it's just...he was such a nice guy."

"So I've heard."

She pulled herself together. "Are you here to look at cars again?"

"Actually, I'm really interested in that yellow Beetle convertible you told me about." I patted the manila folder in my hand. "I've made some notes on cars I like at other dealerships. But I was hoping yours might be out of the shop by now?"

"Not as far as I know."

"Any chance I can see it? Just a quick peek?"

She pulled out her phone. "Let me call Mac in the shop."

Within minutes an orange hulk lumbered through a back entrance, the square face above his coveralls cold and hard as stone.

"Oh, Mac, you didn't need to come out here," Fiona said. "My customer is interested in the Beetle. She'd like to have a quick look at it, if you don't mind."

"Customers are not allowed in the shop," he said. "You know that, Fiona." But he was looking at me. "We're getting it ready to paint."

"Oh, I hope you're not changing the color."

Mac looked at me like I had lost my mind.

"Don't worry," Fiona said. "It's just some minor damage. Right, Mac?"

When Mac didn't seem inclined to answer, I piped up, "Can you tell me if it was in an accident? What sort of damage did it sustain?"

He stared at me a moment longer, turned and stomped away.

"Sorry," Fiona said. "Mac wasn't hired for his people skills."

* * *

After promising to return in a few days, I continued along the sidewalk to a mall several blocks away. My brain kept telling me what I had to do that night, but with each step my every instinct begged me to find a less terrifying option.

Georgia's cash bought me a jacket, turtleneck, yoga pants and a pair of soft-soled boots. All black. I completed my stealth wardrobe with a black baseball cap and skintight black leather gloves.

Next stop was a hardware store, where I selected a set of tools and a zippered case to carry them in. I silently thanked Vern for sharing his expertise in this line of work. At the food court, I ordered a banana smoothie and sat down to review my plans. My burn phone rang and I answered, expecting Georgia.

"Hey, girl, how's it going in the big city?"

The soft-spoken voice sounded familiar, and yet something had changed. "Vern? You sound tense."

After a brief pause he said, "Your sister's nothing like you, is she?"

"Oh-oh, she's driving you nuts, right?"

"The woman wants to buy me a lawn mower."

I stifled a laugh. "Sorry about that, Vern, but I didn't know what else to do with her."

"I might have a few suggestions."

This time I did laugh. "Hang in there. I'm hoping to wrap it up by tonight."

"Good luck, then, Leena girl, but be careful. Don't do anything crazy."

"Hey, you know me. Cautious to a fault."

Unless I can't think of an easy way out, I thought.

* * *

In late afternoon I returned to the restaurant. The lunch crowd had dispersed, and only a few customers lingered over their meals. The same server walked up to me, carrying menus.

"Oh, it's you again," she said. "You're in luck. My manager isn't busy now, and Christie should be here soon."

I spent the next half hour being interviewed for a job I didn't want. When it was finally over, the manager said she'd call me soon. I thanked her.

Christie was just coming on shift. "Hey," she said, "how'd it go?"

"Good. She said she'll call."

"Woo-hoo!" Christie high-fived me. "So, are you hungry? Might as well get familiar with the menu. My treat since you paid last night."

"Yeah, now that you mention it, I'm starving! All I've had today is motel coffee, a stale muffin and a smoothie."

"Say no more." Christie grabbed a menu and led me to a table.

"Anything new on your investigation?" she asked as she poured coffee. "Do you still think she's innocent?"

"Who? Georgia Branson?"

"The police are looking for her, right? Why would she run if she didn't do it?"

I studied her face. An open, honest face. Not the face of a liar or a murderer, attempted or otherwise. Or so I thought, but I needed to be sure. "Mrs. Branson had a very good reason for running. Someone was trying to kill her."

Christie's face paled. She sank onto the seat across from me. "What? Who?"

"According to my source, Mrs. Branson believed it was her husband. She took off before she knew he was dead."

"She's lying. Anyone who knew Mark would know he'd never hurt anyone."

"Mrs. Branson was the victim of a hit and run, a near miss. She saw the car. It was a yellow VW Beetle."

Christie stared at me, eyes wide. "You think it was me?"

"Georgia Branson sustained injuries throwing herself from her bike. The car hit a fire hydrant, damaging the right front fender."

She slapped the table, her voice loud. "So you do think it was me!"

"Okay. I admit, at first I did, but now I'm trying to prove it wasn't you."

She studied my face as I had studied hers. What she saw must have convinced her. She nodded.

"Christie, how long have you had your car?"

"Um…I'm not sure…about six weeks."

"And did Mark ever borrow it?"

"Are you kidding me? That man wouldn't drive anything but his precious little sports car."

"Assuming he had a key, could he have taken your car last Sunday without your knowledge?"

"Sunday? No. That was my day off. I drove up island to visit my parents. I was gone all day."

"Good, then." I outlined what I had learned, what I suspected and what I was about to do.

"Seriously?" she asked. "Are you out of your mind? If you're right, you could get yourself killed."

"I kinda hope not," I said, "but just in case, I'm counting on you to be my backup. Promise you'll go to the police and tell them everything you know?"

She stared at me, mouth hanging open.

"Christie, I'm kidding. I'll be fine. But if you're working this evening, there's one thing you can do to help."

"What's that?"

"Keep your phone close. I may send you some photos."

"As backup," she said.

"You got it."

FOURTEEN

Back at my motel room, I paced the floor. Waiting for dark. Trying to calm my nerves. My hands trembled as I dressed in my new outfit and placed the toolkit in my shoulder bag. For a long moment I stared at my image in the mirror. Then I walked out the door.

The showroom was lit up like day, but the place was deserted. I drove around the building and parked away from the glare of overhead lamps. After pulling on my skin-thin gloves, I grabbed my shoulder bag, complete with my brand-new tools of the trade. Like a cat burglar, I blended into the night.

A commercial trash container stood against the wall beneath a large Scrap Metal sign. I opened the lid and shone my flashlight inside. The bin was a tangle of rusty pipes and bits of wire. Half hidden under a mangled car fender lay a perfectly good crowbar, its hooked end painted fire-hydrant red. The puzzle was fitting together.

I assembled my smartphone, snapped some photos, then moved the crowbar to the top of the pile and took some more, being sure to emphasize the painted end. I moved the camera in for a close-up of several yellow scratches that marred the red. Finally, I stepped back for some shots of the bin that showed the building behind. I carried the crowbar with me to the shop door.

I was in luck. The lock was a simple one. Thanks to Vern's patient tutoring, I knew exactly what to do. I pulled my little toolkit from my handbag and was inside in seconds, heart thundering like a bass drum. I paused, nerves on edge, expecting an alarm to shatter the silence. Breathed again when the shop remained quiet. My flashlight beam sliced through the darkness and landed on a blue tarp covering the front end of the yellow Beetle. I hurried over, yanked it off and stood back, surprised at the extent of the damage. This car needed more than a simple paint job. Mac must be waiting for a new fender to come in.

Putting down the crowbar, I took photos from various angles. Then I sent all the photos to Christie, along with a text message. **If anything happens to me, consider yourself backup.**

Outside, a car door slammed. My stomach clenched. Footsteps approached. Keys jangled. I tossed the tarp back over the car and huddled behind it. Flashlight off. Phone in hand. My heart stopped in mid beat.

My hands shook so hard I almost dropped the phone. I paused, took a deep breath, found Christie's number and pushed Call. It went straight to voice mail.

The lock clicked. The door creaked open.

"Don't phone or text," I whispered. "I might be in trouble here. I'll call back."

I pushed End Call and slipped the smartphone into my jacket pocket.

Lights blared, hurting my eyes. I fumbled for the burn phone in my bag. Found the mini-recorder instead. Turned it on. Then the burn phone. Footsteps echoed on the cement floor. A shadow on the wall grew bigger with every step. The footsteps stopped beside the car. The shadow bent. Picked up the crowbar. Footsteps crunched across the tarp.

Before I could hit 9-1-1 he was on me. He grabbed the burn phone from my hand, ripped it open, pulled out the battery and stomped the phone under his boot. "What are you doing here?" he demanded.

I swallowed. Struggled to speak. "I told you I wanted to see this car." My voice came out bolder than I felt.

Larry's smile was smooth and oily. "Then I suggest we take it for a test drive."

"Now?"

He studied the crowbar in his hand. "There's no time like the present." He selected some keys from a rack and slid them into his jeans pocket. Then, grabbing a chunk of rope from a cluttered work-bench, he yanked me to my feet. His fingers gripped my arm with surprising strength. Larry was mere inches taller than me and maybe thirty pounds heavier, but he must have been all muscle. The harder I fought to get away, the more helpless I felt. His fingers dug deep into muscle, hurting like stink.

"You won't get away with this," I warned him.

That oily smile again. "With what? You asked for a test drive, and I have a note on my calendar to prove it. Here at Russell Volkswagen, we pride ourselves on offering customer service second to none."

"What happened to B&R Volkswagen?"

"Sadly, the B part of the partnership is no longer with us." He chuckled. "To be honest, I never was fond of that name." He steered me toward the passenger door. "Shall we go?"

"Maybe you haven't noticed," I said, "but the dealership is closed. And since I'm meeting a friend for dinner, I'd be happy to come back tomorrow."

"I'm sure you would." The tone of his voice sent fear down my spine.

He opened the passenger door.

"Get in."

"And if I refuse?"

"Your choice." He turned the crowbar over in his hand. "The seat or the trunk—which, you'll be happy to discover, is surprisingly spacious for such a small vehicle."

Cold with fear, I slid into the passenger seat, my bag on my lap. Larry wrapped the rope around my right wrist, pulled it tight enough to hurt and tied it to the hand grip on the door. Clearly, he hadn't thought this through, because when he closed the door the rope went slack.

Larry bent over to retrieve broken bits of phone. I had seconds to act.

I pressed the door lock and then, with my left hand, pulled my smartphone from my pocket. Christie's was the last number called, at the top of the list. I pressed it.

"Please answer! Please answer!" I whispered, clutching the phone to my right ear, away from Larry, who was now at the driver's door.

"Leena? You all right?" Christie's voice in my ear.

Larry tried the door, realized it was locked and fumbled in his pocket for the keys.

"Listen. Don't speak. Larry forced me into yellow Beetle, leaving lot soon. Call 9-1-1. I'll keep my phone on."

The door opened. I shoved the phone deep into the left-hand pocket of my jacket.

"How stupid was that?" Larry fumed, getting in. "As if I didn't have the keys." He leaned over and pressed the crowbar hard across my throat. I gagged, unable to breathe. My eyes bugged. My heart pounded.

"I'd kill you right here, but Mac's just finished cleaning the car." He placed the crowbar beside the driver's door and started the engine. "No one messes with Mac."

The lot was deserted. Lights glowed from lampposts and reflected off rows of windshields as we passed by. Larry stopped at the busy main road, flicked on his turn signal and waited for a break in traffic. Then he turned right, driving past Jamie's Family Restaurant. I glanced sideways. There, in the lighted window, was a welcome face. Phone to her ear, Christie waved a second phone, then spun away.

This woman was no bimbo. Christie must have borrowed a second phone so she could keep the line open.

We continued along the main drag in heavy traffic. Larry stared straight ahead, his expression grim, hands tight on the wheel.

"Where are you taking me?"

He didn't answer.

"Shouldn't I be driving?" I asked, "I mean, since it's a test drive and all?"

He ignored me.

"Why don't you pull into Town Center Mall here so we can switch sides?"

"Why don't you shut up?" he growled.

I did. And listened to my heart pounding in my ears, so fast it didn't leave time for thinking. I looked in my side mirror.

Was that a second yellow Beetle several cars back? A glimpse, and it was gone.

"So, you're going to show me how it handles on the highway," I said a few minutes later. "Good idea." I was afraid to speak too loudly and could only hope the line was still open and Christie could hear.

Larry pressed his foot on the gas and zipped into the left lane, cutting in front of a pickup truck. Its horn blasted.

"What, are you trying to get us both killed?" I asked.

"Do you even know how to stop talking?" he growled. "And who are you really? Why stick your nose where it doesn't belong?"

FIFTEEN

Okay. Good question. Why *do* I stick my nose where it doesn't belong? "What if I told you I'm a private investigator hired by Davida O'Neil?"

His head swiveled my way. "Mark's mother-in-law? Why the hell would she hire you?"

"She doesn't believe her daughter killed Mark. She wants to find out what really happened."

"Good luck with that." He snickered. "Innocent people don't run."

"According to Ms. O'Neil—who happens to be a defense attorney—the police too often zero in on one suspect and ignore any evidence that points to someone else. This time they're convinced that her daughter, Georgia, is guilty, but I've uncovered plenty of evidence that points to you, Larry. You can be sure I've kept Ms. O'Neil informed every step of the way. Including sending photos of this Beetle in your shop, damaged fender and all."

"So what? We took it in on trade that way."

"According to Georgia Branson, someone ran her off the road and damaged their car in the process. Someone driving a yellow VW Beetle." I paused for effect. "I know it was you, Larry."

"And why would I do that, exactly?"

"For the same reason you followed her in the parkade. To scare her into running away. It worked."

"Nice try. Wrong, but good guess. And I don't think you sent any photos before your phone broke."

"It's a free country. Think whatever you want."

He drove for a moment in silence. "Where does she live?"

"Who?"

"You moron. Georgia's mother, of course."

"I have no clue."

"So you're lying. I figured as much."

"Did I say I went to her home? We met at her law offices. And that's where she was when I talked to her just before you showed up."

He went quiet.

"I really don't care what you believe, Larry. But killing me won't make your problems go away."

He swung the wheel hard to the right, cut across a lane of traffic and squealed onto an exit ramp. "Change of plans," he said. "It's time I offered my condolences to Ms. Davida O'Neil on the unfortunate loss of her son-in-law."

"Now who's lying? You have no idea where her office is."

"Oh, but I do, my dear. It was her office that drew up the papers when we purchased the dealership a few years back. Mark and I met with her and Georgia there."

"Don't tell me—let me guess. In the event one partner dies, the other two split his or her share?"

He glanced my way, eyebrows raised.

"And if Georgia is convicted of murder…"

"I'll have sole control of Russell Volkswagen for a very long time. I couldn't let Mark divorce Georgia—we would have been ruined."

"So you killed him."

"I didn't want to. Mark was a good business partner. It was Georgia I wanted to get out of the way."

"So, what, you mistook Mark for Georgia in the park?" I knew he was ready to spill the entire story. First he'd tell me. And then he'd have to kill me. No joke.

"The stupid bitch came in screaming at Mark. Said he'd tried to run her down with his girlfriend's car. After the dealership closed that night, he confronted me."

Sometimes silence works better than words. I waited.

"I told him it must have been Christie." Larry touched the crowbar beside him. "I even bashed her front fender to prove it. The red paint was an inspiration! But Mark wasn't buying. He had seen the damage to the other Beetle in the shop."

"Mark was going to turn you in."

"He should have been grateful. I did it for both of us, for the good of the dealership. I told him I wouldn't miss the next time, and he'd be free of his wife. But the fool threatened to call the cops."

"So you decided to kill him."

"I begged him to let me turn myself in. He gave me until the next morning—a nice guy, but stupid. He left me no choice."

"There's always a choice, Larry."

He glanced in the left mirror. "Shit!"

"What?"

"A yellow Beetle followed us from the highway."

"So? There must be dozens of them around town."

He wheeled onto a side road and stopped. I checked the right hand mirror. Saw the second Beetle continue on past. Larry pulled a U-turn and followed.

The lemon jellybean car beetled along in front of us, weaving through traffic, never letting us close enough to see the driver. A half block ahead, it approached an amber light, zipped into the left lane and ran through just as the light turned red. Larry screeched to a stop behind a Smart car. A streak of yellow disappeared around the next bend.

"Shit!" He slammed his fist against the steering wheel.

* * *

We pulled up in front of O'Neil and Branson without spotting any more yellow Beetles. And trust me, I was watching for them.

Larry got out of the car, taking the crowbar. I peered up at the eighth-floor corner-office window. Light glowed behind closed blinds. Good old Mom, always working late.

A cold, aching fear settled over me. A sense of impending doom. In recent months I had imagined coming home. Reconciling with my mother. But never like this. This would be one hell of a family reunion.

The outside door automatically locked at seven. This I remembered. Larry punched in the number for her office. Seconds later my mother's voice shattered the night air. Cool and direct. As always. "This office is closed."

Larry pushed my face up to the microphone. "Get us in," he hissed.

"Uh…it's me, Mrs. O'Neil. It's Leena."

"Leena?" She sounded confused, as she would be. My mother named me Colleen. She had never called me anything else.

"Yes, ma'am. Leena Swindle? Your investigator?" Surely she would pick up on my father's last name, if not Leena. "I, uh, I have some new information I'm sure will interest you."

There was a long pause, then, breathless, "Something wrong with your phone?"

"Actually"—I glared at Larry—" it kinda broke. But Mrs. O'Neil, trust me, this is important. Something I need to deliver in person."

The door unlocked with a solid clunk. I felt ill.

In the elevator, Larry shifted from one foot to the other. Crowbar clutched in his right hand, he stared at the little lighted numbers as we rose inexorably to the eighth floor.

I closed my eyes, my stomach in turmoil. A thousand questions bounced around my skull. Had Christie overheard where we were headed? Had she managed to contact my mother? The police? Would I live through this night? Would my mother? Why had she never tried to find me? Would she be angry with me for coming here?

The door hissed open.

SIXTEEN

It was a long walk down a long hallway to the office door. *O'Neil and Branson, Attorneys at Law.* The assistant's desk, the open door to her office. Strange and familiar. Her face behind a huge desk, studying her computer screen. Familiar but older. So much older. These last few days must have been hell for her, not knowing where her perfect daughter was.

"Leave the door open," she commanded, not looking up.

Family photos on the wall. The one of me missing, in its place a beige rectangle paler than the surrounding wall. So. She must have just taken my picture down. Smart move, because Larry would have spotted it for sure. And it made me feel just a little better, knowing she had been expecting us. *Thank you, Christie!*

My eyes shifted to Mom's favorite vase—large, heavy, cut crystal—holding a bouquet of yellow chrysanthemums. My favorite flower. Had she picked them from the garden I planted?

Larry's fingers tightened around my upper arm, but he did as commanded. Was even he afraid of her? We stood in front of her desk like schoolchildren. Waiting. She peered over her reading glasses, pale brown eyes cool and appraising. Lioness eyes. Georgia eyes. Unflinching.

I shriveled into my shoes. My mother hadn't shown a glimmer of recognition when I showed up. But what did I expect?

That she'd jump up and embrace her long-lost daughter? That she'd *care*?

But Davida O'Neil cannot be my mother right now, I reminded myself. And I'm not Colleen O'Neil, her disappointing daughter. I'm Leena Swindle, her private investigator.

Okay, then. Where was Christie right now? Was that second yellow Beetle really hers? If she heard everything, could she have beaten us here?

Davida O'Neil's eyes scrolled from Larry's face to his right hand holding the crowbar, to me. "I see you've brought the suspect along," she said, her voice cool. "Or has he brought you?"

Larry's fingers dug deeper into muscle. "Ms. O'Neil, I'll need you to come with us," he said.

She whipped off her glasses. "And why would I want to do that?"

"Because..." His voice was uncertain, as if he was still plotting his next move. "If you don't, I'll kill you both right now."

She stood up slowly, placed both hands on her desk and leaned toward him. "Mr. Russell, if you plan on killing us, I'd prefer you do it right here. Right now. I will not let you cart us off to some remote location where our bodies may never be found. So I suggest you do what you will and take your chances out there." She glanced toward the door. "With blood all over your clothes."

The room went so quiet I could almost hear Larry thinking. Clearly, he was in over his head. Nothing was working out the way he had planned. But could he kill two women in cold blood?

The answer was a chilling *yes*. This man had beat his good friend and business partner to death with Georgia's golf club. Then returned the club to her car, using copies of her keys that he must have made a couple of weeks before. Premeditation.

"Fine," he said, his voice like ice. "Have it your way."

His fingers loosened on my arm. He brandished the crowbar. My mother started around her desk. "Take me first!"

"What's going on here?" The voice came from behind me.

Larry swung around. I pulled away. My mother was a blur of motion.

Christie stood in the doorway, hands on hips, looking scared out of her mind.

"You!" Larry started toward her, crowbar raised.

Everything happened at once. Christie stepped back. I lunged forward, grabbing the crowbar with both hands. Larry tried to wrench it away. I lost my footing. There was a thud and a grunt, and I crumpled to the floor. Something heavy landed on top of me. I realized two things at once.

My fingers were still wrapped around the crowbar, and I was pinned to the carpet by what felt like a dead weight. I wriggled out from under Larry.

Christie still hovered near the door, eyes wide, watching my mother. Mom loomed over Larry's limp body, clutching her crystal vase in both hands. Yellow chrysanthemums and dark puddles of water traced a scattered path back to her desk.

There was a scuffling sound in the hall and then a half dozen police burst into the room, fully geared in helmets, heavy boots and bullet-proof vests. Guns drawn, pointing at me and my mother. "Police! Drop your weapons!"

I looked at the crowbar in my hands. At the vase Mom was holding. Larry moaned, pressing both hands to his head.

My mother turned to the police. "I see you have impeccable timing, as per usual."

"They tried to kill me!" Larry whimpered.

"I don't think so." Christie waved her phone. "You brought Leena here against her will. I heard everything!"

"So there can be no doubts," my mother added, "everything that transpired here this evening is being recorded on my security camera."

"And my mini-recorder," I added. "For backup."

Two cops raised Larry to his feet, hand-cuffed him and led him away. The other cops followed, heads hanging. The game was over, and no one had got to shoot anyone.

* * *

My mother wrapped her arms around me. It felt good.

"How come you never tried to find me?" I asked.

"Because, Colleen, you left a note saying you would contact me when you were ready. I've been waiting for you to be ready. But

I did hire an investigator to make sure you were all right." She pulled back to study my face. "I couldn't handle not knowing—like when your father..." Her voice broke.

"Disappeared," I finished for her. Was that why she looked so much older now? Not only because of Georgia? I suddenly realized how truly difficult the past three years must have been for my mother.

I touched her face. "I'm so sorry, Mom. I forgot all about that note. I should have called."

"Wait a minute here." Christie stepped into the room. "She's your *mother*? You're Georgia's *sister*? You lied about being a private investigator?"

I turned around. "Christie, I told you this was my first case. It is. And I'm *almost* a private investigator. That's no lie."

She glared at me.

"Look, I'm really sorry, Christie, but I needed to get at the truth, and I didn't think you'd talk to me if you knew who I was. The important thing is, we caught the guy who killed Mark, right?"

She frowned. Stepped back.

"The same guy who bashed up your car and tried to implicate you in a hit and run?"

She looked at me sideways.

"Friends?"

"I'll think about it."

"First," my mother said, businesslike as always, "we'll call Georgia and tell her the good news. Then I'm taking you two young women out for a well-earned dinner. Deal?"

"I'm in," I said, looking at Christie.

"This is too weird," she said. She pressed her fingertips to her forehead. Glanced from me to my mother and back again. Then, quite unexpectedly, she laughed. "But, hey, why not? I never turn down a free meal—only let's not go to Jamie's Family Restaurant."

"It's a deal," I said and grabbed my phone to call my sister.

AUTHOR'S NOTE

You can't judge a person by their appearance. The mild-mannered woman seated across from you on the ferry might well be plotting her next murder. An almost perfect murder. One that will slowly unravel, given a determined investigator like Leena O'Neil. Leena sprang to life with this, her first case to solve. She plans on being around for many more.

DAYLE CAMPBELL GAETZ has worked as a creative writing instructor, book editor and columnist but now devotes her time to her own writing. Gaetz is the author of over twenty books for young people and adults. Her 2013 novel *Taking the Reins* won a Moonbeam Gold Award for historical fiction and a Willa Literary Award. Gaetz grew up in Victoria, British Columbia, enjoyed twenty-two years on Salt Spring Island and now lives in Campbell River.

Meet the
Goddaughter...

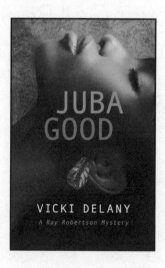

RCMP Sergeant Ray Robertson has spent nearly a
year serving with the United Nations in South Sudan.
He can't wait to get back home, back to policing a
world he understands. But when a young woman—
the fourth in three weeks—is found dead, Robertson
fears that a serial killer is on the loose. It's up to him
and his Sudanese partner, John Deng, to find the
killer before they can strike again.

Juba Good is the first in a series of mysteries
featuring RCMP Sergeant Ray Robertson.

"A page-turner filled with suspense. The characters are
true to life as is the setting. Highly Recommended."
—*CM Magazine*

RAPID READS
WWW.RAPID-READS.COM

Discover Gail Bowen's Charlie D Mysteries

Charlie D is the host of a successful late-night radio call-in show, *The World According to Charlie D.* Each of these novels features a mystery that is played out in a race against time as Charlie D fights to save the innocent and redeem himself.

Amanda Moss is a young hairstylist with ambitions to become a musician and play in a band. One day her life changes dramatically when a stranger shows up and tells Amanda that her real mother has just died of cancer while serving a life sentence for the murder of Amanda's father. Suddenly Amanda feels her whole life has been a lie.

"Well-written...this novel features believable characters, a taut plot and a satisfying ending. A quick read, and a book the reader will not be able to put down."

—*Tri State YA Book Review Committee*

RAPID READS
WWW.RAPID-READS.COM